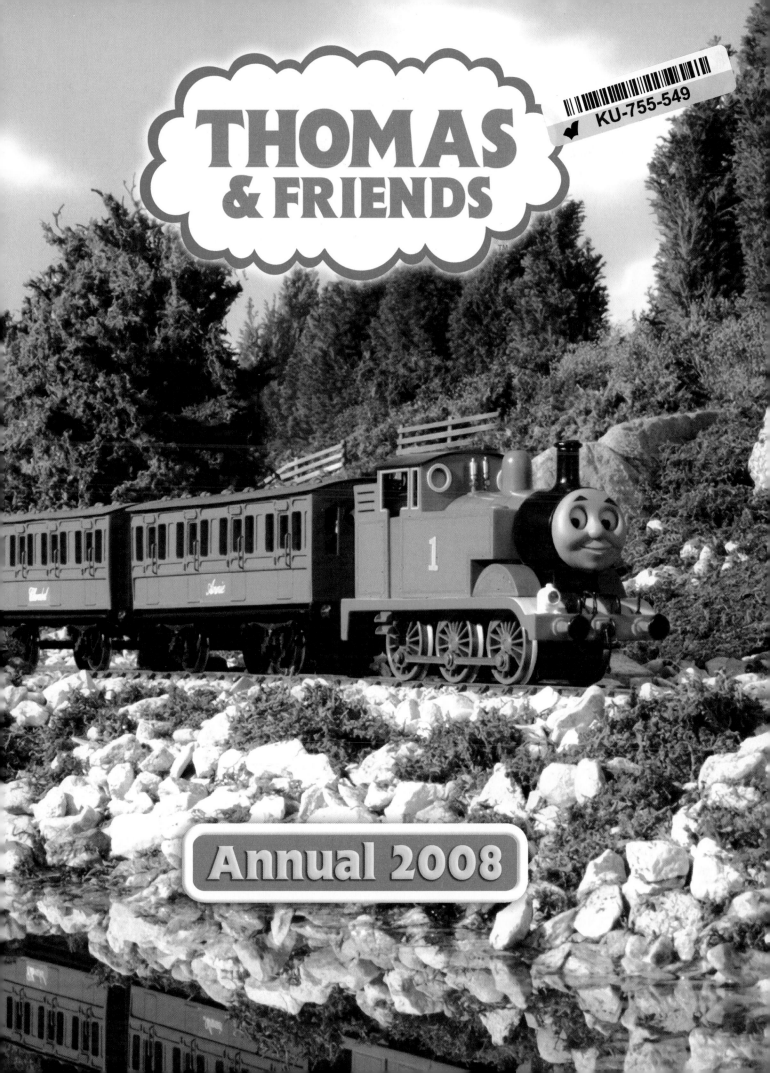

THOMAS & FRIENDS™

Annual 2008

Contents

HiT entertainment

Thomas the Tank Engine & Friends

A BRITT ALLCROFT COMPANY PRODUCTION

Based on The Railway Series by The Rev W Awdry

© Gullane (Thomas) LLC 2007

Photographs © Gullane (Thomas) Limited 2007

EGMONT

We bring stories to life

First published in Great Britain 2007 by Egmont UK Limited
239 Kensington High Street, London W8 6SA

ISBN 978 1 4052 3168 8

10 9 8 7 6 5 4 3 2 1

Printed in Italy

Stories based on original scripts by Abi Grant, Paul Larson, Sharon Miller, Simon Nicholson and Marc Seal.

This annual belongs to:

_____

Peep!

"Hello, everyone! Welcome to the Island of Sodor. I hope you enjoy reading all about me and my very special engine friends!"

Thomas' railway ABC

"**Peep!** This **ABC** alphabet starts at **A** for Annie and ends at **Z** for **ZZZZ**, the noise that sleeping engines make!"

A is for **Annie**, one of my coaches. She works on my Branch Line with Clarabel. We take workmen to and from the Quarry.

B is for **Bill and Ben**. They are twins who work on the line from the Clay Pits to the Harbour.
B is also for **Brendam Docks**.

C is for **Cranky** the crane. He works at the Docks, loading and unloading from ships and trains.

C is also for **Clarabel**.

D is for **Duncan**, the gold Number 6 engine who works on the Narrow Gauge Railway. His story is on page 22.

E is for **Emily**, a little green engine.

E is also for **Edward**, the kind blue Number 2.

F is for *The Fat Controller*.

He is in charge of the Railway. Do you know his real name? Yes, it's Sir Topham Hatt.

G is for **Gordon**, Number 4.

He's the fastest engine and pulls the big Express.

H is for **Henry**, the green Number 3 engine.

H is for **Harvey** the crane engine and for **Harold** the helicopter, too.

I is for the **Island** of Sodor. Lots of people visit to ride on the Railway.

J is for **James**, the red Number 5 engine.

J is also for **Jeremy** the jet plane. Read his story on page 30.

K is for **Knapford Station**. We go there with passengers and goods.

L is for **Lady Hatt**. She's married to The Fat Controller and comes to visit us sometimes.

M is for **Maithwaite**, a very busy station, and for **Mighty Mac**, a Narrow Gauge engine.

MAITHWAITE

N is for the **Narrow Gauge engines**. Their names are Duncan, Rusty, Peter Sam, Rheneas, Sir Handel, Skarloey and Mighty Mac.

O is for **Oliver**, the green Number 11 tank engine. His brake van is called Toad.

P is for **Percy**, the little green Number 6 engine, and my best friend.

P is also for **Peter Sam**, who always works hard.

Q is for the **Quarry**. It's at one end of my Branch Line and I take the men there and bring them back every day.

R is for **Rusty**, the Number 5 diesel engine and for **Rheneas**, the little Number 2 engine.

S is for **Salty**, who shunts the trains at Brendam Docks.

S is also for **Skarloey** and **Sir Handel**, two of the Narrow Gauge engines on the Mountain Railway.

T is for **The Thin Controller**. His real name is Mr Percival, and he runs the Narrow Gauge Railway.

T is also for **Toby** the Number 7 tram engine, and for **Troublesome Trucks**.

U is for **Useful**, which is what all the engines want to be – especially me!

V is for **Viaduct**, a bridge with lots of arches. Skarloey likes it because it's high up in the air!

W is for the **Wharf**. Read about how Skarloey got on there on page 50.

X is for **Xroads**. It's the crossroads where the engines must wait if the signal is down.

Y is for **Yellow**, the colour of Bill and Ben – and The Fat and Thin Controllers' waistcoats!

Z is for **ZZZZ**. It's the noise you hear coming from the Engine Shed at night, when we're all fast asleep!

Thomas and the treasure

Brendam Docks is a very busy place. Engines move goods trucks there, cranes unload cargo, and ships bring visitors.

One day, Thomas went there to collect a very important visitor – the Admiral! He was going to open the new Maritime Museum, and Thomas was taking him there.

Salty said, "I've seen the Admiral before. He comes to Sodor to look for the pirate treasure that's hidden here!"

"Pirates?" said James.

"Treasure?" said Emily.

"Rubbish!" said Henry.

"Oh, yes," said Salty. "There's pirate treasure here, but no one has ever found it!"

Salty told them more. "There are three clues that lead to the treasure," he said. "First, find the **eagle of the mountains**. Its beak points to the **clouds that are not in the sky**. They show the way to the **skull and crossbones**! And there you'll find the treasure, me hearties!"

Emily and James thought Salty was being silly!

But Thomas didn't. "Eagle … clouds … skull and crossbones …" he tooted. "I'm sure I can find those clues!"

Thomas puffed off. "What if I get to the Museum with the Admiral and a chest of pirate treasure?" he said. "That will show the others!"

Naughty Thomas chuffed along a track that went to the mountains. He was going to look for the first clue!

"Where will I find an eagle?" said Thomas. "How can clouds not be in the sky? And where will I find a skull and crossbones?"

Later, Emily puffed up to Thomas. "There's no buried treasure!" she laughed.

But Thomas took no notice of her.

Suddenly, Thomas saw a mountain that was shaped like an eagle!

"I've found the first clue!" he peeped happily. "Salty said the eagle's beak points to the next one!"

There was a track in front of the stone beak so Thomas chuffed along it.

James saw him. "Where are you going, Thomas?" he wheeshed.

"To find the clouds that are not in the sky!" whistled Thomas.

James snorted. "Oh, how silly!"

Thomas didn't care, because he soon found the clouds! They weren't in the sky. They were reflections in the lake!

"Peep!" said Thomas. "The second clue! I need to solve one more to find the treasure!"

Thomas searched and searched. He forgot all about the Admiral! He was still looking when Harold arrived with The Fat Controller.

"The Admiral is late for the opening of the Maritime Museum!" The Fat Controller told Thomas. "You have been unreliable. Harold will take him now."

Thomas felt bad. He knew he had spent too much time looking for clues.

"Fancy believing in a silly old story!" laughed Harold.

"Everyone thinks I'm silly," huffed Thomas. "But I still believe in the treasure!"

He puffed along the track that led away from the lake. He had never been this way before. He didn't know that it led into … a tunnel!

Thomas chuffed through it and came out at the Maritime Museum!

"I am proud to open the Maritime Museum!" said the Admiral.

Everyone cheered. **"Peep!"** said Thomas. "The pirate treasure is here!"

"Don't be silly, Thomas!" huffed Emily.

"It's just a silly old story!" snorted James.

But Thomas knew he was right. "Look at the rocks! It's the skull and crossbones!" he puffed.

"Yes!" said the Admiral. "Someone get me a shovel!"

The Admiral dug down into the sand and found a big wooden chest. Inside there were jewels and pearls and lots of gold coins.

"The treasure will be the most important thing in the whole Maritime Museum!" said the Admiral.

"Well done, Thomas," said The Fat Controller.

Thomas felt very proud. He had been right to believe Salty's story! He had found the pirate treasure!

Spot the difference

The other engines didn't believe Salty when he told them about the pirate treasure.

"Rubbish!" said Henry.

But Thomas believed him – and he found the treasure!

1

These two pictures look the same, but there are 5 things that are different in picture 2.

Look carefully – can you spot them all?

(2)

Duncan drops a clanger

It was a busy time on the Narrow Gauge Railway. The little engines were helping to get things ready for the big County Fair. They all had jobs to do.

Rusty was taking trucks full of flowers.

Peter Sam was taking big pumpkins.

Duncan had a very special job. He was collecting the big bell from the clock tower and taking it to be polished.

On his way to collect the bell, he puffed along an old track. It was rough and bumpy, but Duncan loved rattling along. **Clickety-clack!** He liked the sound his wheels made so he raced along going **rattle! clatter!** over the bumps. When he got to the end of the track he went back and did it again!

"You're going to be late!" said Rheneas.

But Duncan didn't hear him. **Clitter-clatter!** His wheels were making too much noise!

When Duncan got to the Transfer Yards, he was very late.

The Foreman was cross. The workmen were all waiting for him. They loaded a big wooden frame with the bell in it on to Duncan's flatbed.

Dong! went the bell.

"What a lovely sound!" peeped Duncan.

"Now remember," said the Foreman, "the bell is very heavy and the track that goes to the polisher's workshop is old. You must go very **slowly** and **carefully**."

But Duncan wasn't listening to the Foreman. **Dong!** He was listening to the bell.

Duncan chuffed along happily. His wheels clattered and the bell rang loudly.

He went faster and the bell chimed louder still: **dong! dong! dong!**

The bell rang and clanged with every bump and bend in the track.

Duncan was having fun.

"Wheee!" he said, happily.

Duncan went faster and faster and the bell rang louder and louder: **dong! dong! dong!**

"Slow down!" said Rusty.

But Duncan didn't hear him. The bell was making too much noise.

"Take care!" chuffed Skarloey.

But Duncan didn't hear him, either.

"The bell will come loose!" puffed Mighty Mac.

But still Duncan didn't hear.

Sir Handel was taking on water when Duncan rattled past him. "Slow down!" said Sir Handel. "The track is very wobbly."

Duncan should have listened to what he said. His wheels rattled over the wobbly track. He put on his brakes, but it was too late. **Bump! clang! bong! clong!** The flatbed lifted into the air and the bell fell off and rolled down the hill:

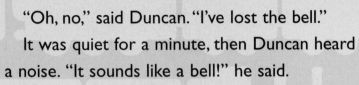

"Oh, no," said Duncan. "I've lost the bell."

It was quiet for a minute, then Duncan heard a noise. "It sounds like a bell!" he said.

It **WAS** a bell! "If I follow the sound I'll find the bell," said Duncan.

Duncan followed the sounds. They got louder and louder until ... Duncan saw the bell. But it was caught on a tree branch!

Duncan raced along and stopped under the bell. The wind blew it this way and that, this way and that ... then the branch snapped!

Duncan was just in time and the bell fell on to his flatbed: **dong!**

"Hooray!" chuffed Duncan.

He set off to the polisher's workshop again. But this time he went very **slowly** and **carefully**, just as he had been told to.

Soon the bell was polished and shiny again. Duncan took it back to the Transfer Yards making sure that he went **slowly** and **carefully**.

Duncan delivered the shiny bell just in time. He heard it ring as the clock chimed to open the County Fair. *Clang! Clang! Clang!* It was the best sound he had ever heard!

Just in time!

When Duncan took the bell back to the big clock he didn't clatter along. He went **slowly** and **carefully**, and he got there just in time.

The big picture is from Duncan's story. Which of the little pictures on this page can you see in the big one?

Write ✔ for yes or ✗ for no in each flag.

1

2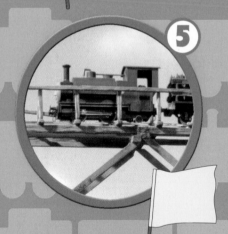

3

4

5

6

7

8

9

10

ANSWERS: Pictures 1, 2, 3, 6, 7 and 10 are part of the big picture. Pictures 4, 5, 8 and 9 are not.

29

Thomas and the jet plane

Thomas loves having buffers that **biff** and **bash** and a boiler that **bubbles**. He loves having **clickety-clackety** wheels and a whistle that goes **peep**.

But most of all Thomas loves being a Really Useful Engine on The Fat Controller's railway.

On the day of the Sodor Summer Picnic, The Fat Controller had a special job for him.

"I want you to collect the children from the Airport and bring them to the picnic," he said.

"Yes, Sir!" said Thomas.

He set off right away.

The Airport was new and all the engines wanted to go there. Thomas was pleased that he had been chosen.

When he got there, he heard a loud noise. **Whoosh!** A big jet plane was coming in to land!

"Peep!" said Thomas, and he chuffed over to say hello. "I'm Thomas," he said. "I'm a tank engine."

"Hello," said the plane. "I'm Jeremy. I'm a jet plane."

"Flying must be wonderful," said Thomas.

"Oh, it is!" said Jeremy. "I can go anywhere I like! Anywhere!"

"I like travelling on tracks," Thomas huffed. "I puff past farms and villages."

"But when I'm up in the air I can see the whole Island all at once!" Jeremy boasted.

Thomas took the children to the picnic. He thought Jeremy was a bit of a show-off. "I never want to talk to that jumped-up jet plane again!" he huffed.

Thomas went round a bend in the track and had to stop at a signal.

Whoosh! Jeremy flew right over his funnel!

"It's not fair!" huffed Thomas. "Jeremy doesn't have have to stop at signals."

Thomas puffed away but soon had to stop as there was a cow on the tracks in front of him! He put on his brakes sharply.

"It's not fair," said Thomas. "Jet planes don't have to stop for cows."

Everyone had a good time at the picnic. Everyone but Thomas …

"What's wrong?" asked his friend, Percy, who puffed up beside Thomas.

"Planes can go wherever they like. I can't. I wish I was a jet plane," said Thomas.

"But engines can pull carriages, and take children to picnics," peeped Percy. "Engines are Really Useful!"

But Thomas wasn't so sure ...

Jeremy flew to the Mainland. But when big black clouds filled the sky he had to go back to the Airport. It wasn't safe to fly.

Thomas was chuffing past the Airport when Jeremy landed. Thomas didn't want to talk to him.

But Jeremy said, "Thomas! There's a big rain storm coming. The children's picnic will be ruined!"

"Cinders and ashes!" cried Thomas. "I'll tell The Fat Controller!"

Thomas got to the picnic just in time. "Quick!" he peeped. "There's a big rain storm coming. Pack up the picnic!"

The children packed up the food and sat in Thomas' coaches, Annie and Clarabel.

The picnic was over. Or was it? Thomas had an idea! He puffed back to the Airport. "Can the children have their picnic in your big hangar?" he asked Jeremy.

"Of course they can!" said Jeremy. "Come in!"

The children had a lovely time. And so did The Fat Controller.

"Well done Thomas and Jeremy!" he said. "You have saved the picnic. You are both Really Useful!"

Thomas felt very proud. So did Jeremy!

The picnic

The children enjoyed The Fat Controller's picnic – until a storm came! So Thomas took everything to Jeremy's hangar. Thomas and Jeremy saved the picnic!

The jigsaw puzzle pieces are all mixed up!
Which of the pieces will complete the big picnic picture?
You can draw and colour them in if you like.

Big strong Henry

You can help read this story about Henry. The little pictures will help you. When you see the pictures of Henry and his friends, say their names.

Henry   Thomas   Gordon

Percy   Emily   The Fat Controller

Winter was coming. A farmer built a big

shed for his cows, to keep them warm.

"I need a strong engine to take bricks and

concrete for him," said .

 and  are both strong.

"I'm the strongest!" said ,

so 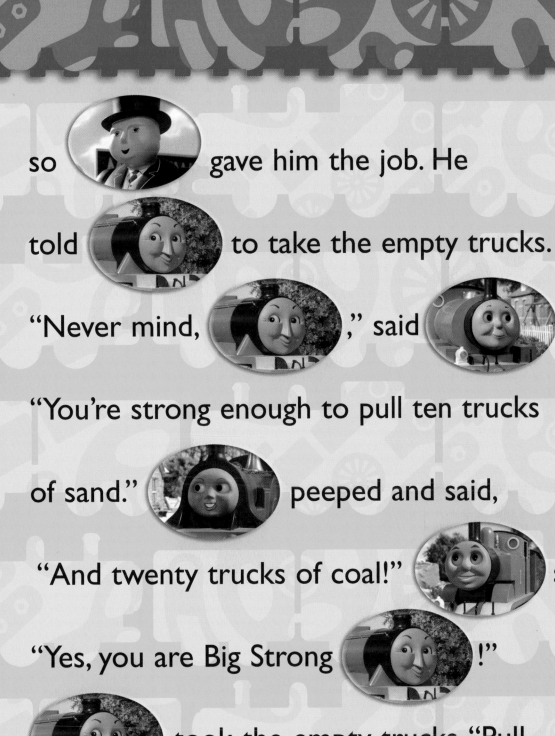 gave him the job. He

told to take the empty trucks.

"Never mind, ," said .

"You're strong enough to pull ten trucks

of sand." peeped and said,

"And twenty trucks of coal!" said,

"Yes, you are Big Strong !"

took the empty trucks. "Pull

the heavy hay trucks to show

how strong you are!" said .

 did, but there was trouble.

The trucks were too heavy. They rolled

away! "Help!" cried  as he ran

off the track.  was cross. He told

 to take the trucks back one

at a time.  told

he could take the cows to their new shed.

 got ready. But the truck doors

were open! "The cows are running away,

!" said .

 let the cows eat hay in his truck.

It gave him an idea!  went very

slowly. The cows followed so they could eat

more hay. They followed clever

all the way to their new shed!

That night  said, "Sorry we got

you in trouble, ."  hooted.

"I shouldn't have tried being Big Strong

!" he said.  said, "You

are Very Helpful  instead!"

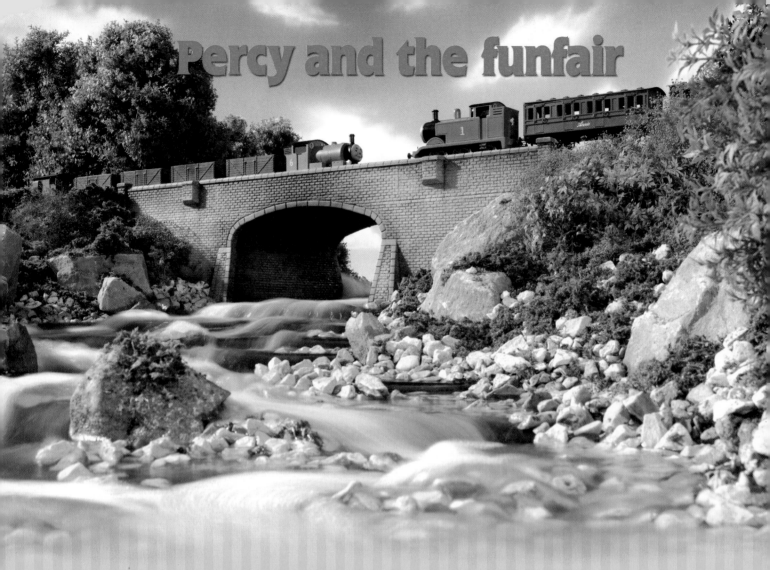

Percy and the funfair

The engines were excited. It was the day of The Fat Controller's funfair and all the children were coming to enjoy the rides.

There was lots to do! The Fat Controller went to Tidmouth to give the engines their jobs.

"Edward, you bring the merry-go-round," said The Fat Controller. "Henry, you can look after the roller-coaster. Gordon will bring the funfair people and Toby will collect the bumper cars. James and Emily will pull the big ferris wheel."

Thomas wondered what his job would be. "Thomas, I want you to collect the fireworks and the Chinese Dragon!" said The Fat Controller.

"What's my job, Sir?" asked Percy.

"I want you to collect coal from the Coaling Plant, Percy," said The Fat Controller. "You must fill the hoppers at all the stations. A railway can't run without coal! This is a Very Important job."

Percy didn't think so! "Coal …" he sighed as he watched his friends steam away.

Percy felt left out as he chuffed to the Coaling Plant. Collecting coal was dull. "I wish I was pulling something exciting," he grumbled. "Not boring old coal trucks!"

Percy buffered up, then pulled out of the depot.

He stopped at the signal near the school playground.

Toby puffed past pulling the bumper cars. The children clapped and cheered when they saw him.

Then Edward chuffed by with the merry-go-round. The children cheered even louder.

Seeing his friends gave Percy an idea. "Toby and Edward need help!" he said. "Helping friends is more important than delivering coal!"

Naughty Percy didn't deliver the coal! He left his trucks and steamed after his friends.

He caught up with Toby and Edward at a red signal.

"Do you need some help?" Percy peeped.

"No thank you, Percy," said Toby.

"We can do it!" chuffed Edward.

"Oh," said Percy.

Further up the line Percy saw Emily and James with the ferris wheel.

"I'm sure they need some help!" he peeped.

He caught up with Emily and James. But they said they didn't need any help.

Gordon was waiting at a junction with the funfair workers when Percy puffed up to him. But Gordon didn't need any help either.

Percy saw Henry on the bridge with the roller-coaster. But he didn't need any help.

Thomas was waiting at a signal when Percy puffed up. Thomas was carrying the fireworks and the big Chinese Dragon. But he didn't need Percy's help.

Percy felt sad and unwanted. Then there was trouble …

The engines needed more coal. But Percy hadn't delivered it!

"There's no coal at the stations!" James told him. "We've all run out!"

"Bust my boiler!" cried Percy. "If the engines don't get coal, there won't be a funfair, and it's all my fault!"

Percy knew what he had to do. He picked up his trucks and took coal to all the stations on Sodor. He went as fast as his wheels would carry him.

Soon all his friends' boilers were bubbling and their pistons were pounding again. The engines were **back on track!**

Percy did his last delivery and got to the funfair just in time to see the fireworks. Rockets soared, the band played, and the Chinese Dragon danced.

Everyone had a lovely time!

"The Fat Controller was right," peeped Percy happily. "Delivering the coal **was** a Very Important job."

Jobs for the engines

The Fat Controller had jobs for all the engines.
Percy's job was to take coal to the stations. Percy didn't
think so at first, but it was a Very Important job!

Which things did the engines take to the funfair? Write ✔ for yes or ✗ for no in each box.

1. Edward took the merry-go-round.

2. Percy took the fireworks and the Chinese Dragon.

3. Henry took the roller-coaster.

4. Toby took the funfair people.

5. Thomas took the bumper cars.

6. James and Emily took the ferris wheel.

Wharf and peace

Skarloey is a happy little engine. He likes puffing past the big blue lake. He likes chuffing across the old bridge, high up in the air.

Sometimes Skarloey has to go to the Wharf. It's near the canal, where roads and railway tracks meet. It's a busy, noisy place, and Skarloey doesn't like it. He feels very small there. He doesn't know anybody's name.

One day, Skarloey pulled some flour trucks to the Wharf. He didn't say hello to anyone and no one said hello to him.

The Troublesome Trucks made fun of him. They wiggled and giggled and biffed him.

When some pipes dropped from a crane they made a loud **clang** and Skarloey jumped. His trucks hit the buffers and flour went everywhere!

"Fancy jumping like that!" said James. "Scaredy little engine!"

Poor Skarloey. He felt smaller than ever.

"Scaredy, scaredy engine!" sang the trucks. "Clickety-clack, don't come back!"

"Maybe I am a scaredy little engine," said Skarloey as he steamed away.

Skarloey collected a bull to take to the Wharf. He felt worried when he came to a rickety bridge, and stopped.

Rusty was at the other side. He didn't like the bridge, either. It was very high up! "What should I do?" he asked.

"I'm not a brave engine," puffed Skarloey. "I don't look down and I puff as hard as I can."

Skarloey showed Rusty how to cross the bridge.

"Thank you, Skarloey!" said Rusty, and he crossed safely.

Skarloey met Duncan. A stream had burst its banks and there was water on the tracks. "If I go in the water it might put out my firebox!" said Duncan. "What should I do?"

"I'm not a brave engine," puffed Skarloey. "I roll very slowly and try not to make any waves."

Skarloey showed Duncan how to go through the water slowly and carefully.

Duncan did just as he said. "Thank you!" he said.

Skarloey was nearly at the Wharf when there was trouble! Runaway logs rolled down the hill from the mill. **Rumble!**

Tumble! Rumble!

Rheneas was coming the other way. "Oh, no!" cried Skarloey. "The logs will hit him!"

Skarloey peeped, but Rheneas didn't hear him. So Skarloey steamed off as fast as he could. The logs hit Skarloey instead, *boof!*

Rheneas said, "Thank you, Skarloey! But why are you so sad?"

"I jumped when I heard a noise at the Wharf," said Skarloey. "The trucks laughed at me and James called me a scaredy little engine. And scaredy engines will never be Useful!"

"But you saved me from the logs!" said Rheneas. "Rusty said you helped him with the bridge. You helped Duncan, too. You are the bravest little engine I know!"

But Skarloey still didn't feel brave. And he still had to go to the Wharf …

When he got there it was as noisy as ever. Then he remembered what Rheneas had said.

"I helped Rusty and Duncan and Rheneas!" he said to himself. "I am a brave little engine!"

He took a big brave puff and said, "Hello everyone, I'm Skarloey!"

The men waved and said, "Hello Skarloey!"

Skarloey was very pleased!

"Clickety-clack, look who's back!" sang the Troublesome Trucks. "The scaredy engine's on our track."

"I am **not** a scaredy engine!" said Skarloey. "And if you biff me, I'll biff you back!"

"Oh!" said the trucks. That shut them up!

Soon the bull was unloaded.

"Good work, Skarloey!" chuffed James.

"You are a Really Useful Engine!" said Thomas.

Skarloey felt very proud, very happy – and very, very brave!

Count with Thomas

Skarloey didn't like the Wharf at first. He felt small there, and none of the men said hello to him.

Colour in a shape for each man you can see in the picture. Count the men, and write the number in the box.

Skarloey was very brave when the logs rolled down the hill. He stopped them hitting his friend, Rheneas.

Colour in a log for each one you can see in the picture. Count the logs, and write the number in the box.

Thomas' frosty friend

Winter is a very busy time on the Island of Sodor. The engines work hard, even when the railway tracks are covered in snow.

Percy has lots of mail to deliver. Gordon carries lots of passengers on the Express. Thomas is busy, too!

One morning he went to Brendam Docks. "I must pick up the logs for Farmer McColl," he puffed.

Thomas met his friend Percy at the signal. He was very excited. "Look what's over there, Thomas!" he peeped. The children had a huge snowman!

"I've never seen such a big one!" said Percy.

"**Peep!** Neither have I!" said Thomas.

When the signal changed to green Thomas steamed away.

Suddenly the wind lifted the snowman right off the ground! Thomas didn't see its ropes get caught on his buffers. He didn't know the snowman was travelling along with him!

Thomas stopped at the level crossing. Suddenly, the snowman bobbed around in front of him. Thomas didn't know it was a balloon. He thought it was a real snowman!

"What are you doing here, Mr Snowman?" cried Thomas. "You must go back! The children will miss you!"

Thomas raced away from the crossing. "If I go very fast the snowman won't be able to keep up with me!" he chuffed.

Thomas met James at Brendam Docks. "Thomas, what are you doing with that snowman?" James said.

"Oh no, he's still here!" said Thomas. "Mr Snowman, I told you to go back to the children! Why are you still following me?"

Thomas steamed off as quickly as he could. He hoped the snowman wouldn't follow him.

"Why have you got that giant balloon tied to your buffers?" called James. But Thomas didn't hear him.

Wheesh!

Thomas stopped at the station. Farmer McColl said, "What are you doing with that snowman, Thomas?"

"Oh no!" tooted Thomas. "Mr Snowman, please go back to the children! Why are you still following me?"

Thomas steamed off as quickly as he could. He hoped the snowman wouldn't follow him.

"Thomas!" called Farmer McColl. "Why have you got that giant balloon tied to your buffers?" But Thomas didn't hear him.

Thomas had to stop at the signal at Maithwaite Station. Emily was there, picking up passengers.

"What are you doing with that snowman?" said Emily.

The wind blew the snowman. He bobbed and bounced around in front of Thomas again.

"Mr Snowman, I told you to go back to the children!" cried Thomas. "Why are you still following me?"

Thomas steamed off as quickly as he could. He hoped the snowman wouldn't follow him. But he did!

Poor Thomas! He didn't know how to make the snowman go back to the children!

Then he had an idea! "I'll hide from him," he whispered.

Thomas chuffed into a lonely siding. The snowman was behind him. Thomas couldn't see him. "I think he's gone back to the children," he tooted.

Suddenly, the wind blew the snowman in front of Thomas again! He was still following him! "I must tell The Fat Controller about this," cried Thomas. "I need his help!"

Thomas raced to Maithwaite Station. Farmer McColl and The Fat Controller were there.

"Please, Sir," peeped Thomas. "I don't know what to do. I told the snowman to go back to the children. But he won't stop following me!"

"I can see that!" laughed The Fat Controller. "The snowman is a balloon, Thomas. His ropes are caught on your buffers. He's not following you. You are pulling him along!"

"A balloon?" whistled Thomas. "I thought snowmen were made of snow."

"Not this one!" said The Fat Controller.

Thomas took his Frosty Friend back to the children. They waved and clapped when they saw Thomas chuffing along with him, and untied his ropes.

"Bye, Mr Snowman!" tooted Thomas. "You won't follow me this time, will you?"

The balloon bobbed around from side to side.

"Peep!" said Thomas. "I think that means NO!"

Mr Snowman

Did you enjoy the story about Thomas' Frosty Friend?
Try these questions. The answers are all in the story!

1. What time of year was it? Spring, summer, autumn or winter?

2. What did Thomas have to collect for Farmer McColl?

3. Who showed Thomas the snowman balloon?

4. Which engine did Thomas meet at Brendam Docks?

5. Which engine was picking up passengers at Maithwaite Station?

Thomas met four of his engine
friends on the day when
Mr Snowman got tied to his buffers.

Can you remember who they were?
Yes, he met ...

EMILY **GORDON** **JAMES** **PERCY**

Can you find
their names in
the word puzzle?
They are spelled
out from left to
right and from
top to bottom.

A	V	P	Z	L	Y	A	Y
A	V	P	Z	L	Y	A	Y
T	B	E	M	I	L	Y	Y
G	O	R	D	O	N	S	S
X	C	C	E	P	M	M	M
D	R	Y	Q	X	S	N	N
W	J	A	M	E	S	O	O

ANSWER:

65

Draw with Thomas

Draw a picture of my Frosty Friend, Mr Snowman, on the next page.

Colour in your picture, then write your name on the line.

1. Draw a big circle for his body and a small circle for his head.

2. Draw 2 arms and mittens.

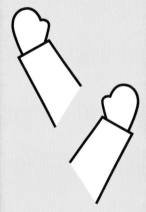

3. Draw a hat, a bow tie and 3 buttons.

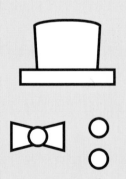

4. Draw 2 eyes, a smiley mouth – and a big red nose!

Mr Snowman by

Thomas' song

Have fun singing this song about
Thomas and his friends.

They're two, they're four, they're six, they're eight,
Shunting trucks and hauling freight,
Red and green and brown and blue,
They're the Really Useful crew.
All with different roles to play
Round Tidmouth Sheds or far away,
Down the hills and round the bends,
Thomas and his friends.

Thomas he's the cheeky one,
James is vain but lots of fun.
Percy pulls the mail on time,
Gordon thunders down the line.
Emily really knows her stuff,
Henry toots and huffs and puffs.
Edward wants to help and share,
Toby, well let's say – he's square!

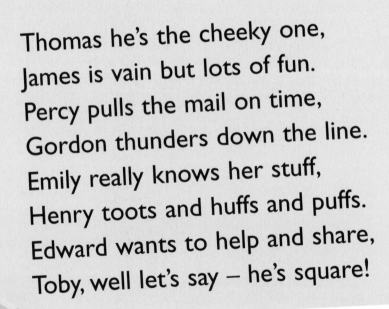

Peep! Goodbye,
see you next year!

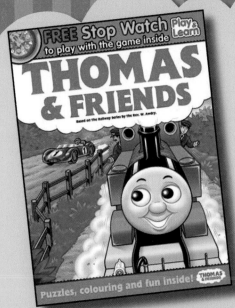
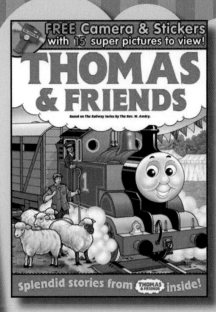
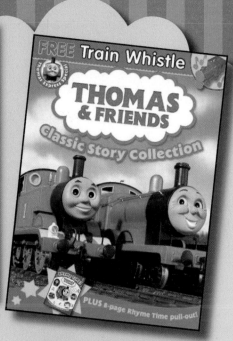